THE SPHINX

/ FROM THE BEGINNING OF TIME

DENISE LEATHEM

 www.trafford.com

North America & international
toll-free: 1 888 232 4444 (USA & Canada)
phone: 250 383 6864 ♦ fax: 812 355 4082

Contents

The Sphinx

From The Beginning of Time

*This book is dedicated to my dear friend Gloria,
who supported me to write this book.*

Acknowledgements

A special thanks to Harold, the love of my life and my life partner, for his encouragement, love and support.

My children Angeline, Coral, and Glen for their faith in me, and last but not least, James Ryan who brought to my attention my ability to become a writer, helping to encourage me when I was ready to give up.

About the Author

Denise Leathem has achieved an Hon. Professorship in Theology, and an Hon. Professorship in Music Harmony and Musicality. She is a qualified therapist in the following subjects: Music, Trauma, Relaxing, Hypnotherapy, Psychology, and Psychiatry. She has obtained a Masters / Teachers and Usui Do in Reiki Minister of Religion, Holistic Healer, and Mystics. Denise currently teaches beginners Piano, Violin and Guitar. She is an accomplished Opera singer and still sings in concerts and does recitals. She has sung in Operas with N.A.P.A.C. Denise is presently writing her fourth book.

THE SPHINX

I t was a beautiful, sunny Wednesday, and I rushed through my daily chores so that I could take advantage of the perfect weather. I was alone at my house and my husband wouldn't be home until after ten p.m. as he attended a board meeting on Wednesday afternoons, which was followed by a dinner for the members. This was the perfect time for me to meditate, and I did so diligently every Wednesday.

I drew the curtains, lit a candle and incense, then settled comfortably into my favourite chair and relaxed. Breathing deeply and imagining myself in a beautiful place, I experienced a sensation of being afloat.

Suddenly, I found myself in an orchard. I looked up into the tall trees and noticed a type of fruit that I couldn't identify; yet, I instinctively knew that it would be safe to eat them. "How on earth am I going to pick some of that fruit?" I thought. The idea had barely registered before I felt my body levitate, floating higher and higher until I hovered in front of the ripest fruit on the tree. I reached forward, intending to pick what resembled a golden pear, and was astonished that the fruit detached itself from the branch and floated into my hand. "Wow!" I exclaimed. "This is amazing; how did that happen?"

I floated to the ground and ate my fruit. It was delicious, and tasted like something that was a cross between mango and pear. Sitting beneath the tree, I looked at the far hills and wondered if it was possible to walk there. Immediately, I was airborne and gliding towards the hills. After landing, I became aware that I wasn't alone. I saw people floating through the nearby treetops. "If we can go anywhere just by thinking, this has got to be a dream," I thought. "Where am I?" I asked aloud.

A voice from among the trees replied, "Atlantis".

"Who said Atlantis?" I asked. I was experiencing a strong sense of déjà vu—I was certain I had been here before but could not pinpoint when. The more I looked around, the more familiar everything seemed.

"I did," the voice answered.

"Let me see who you are," I pleaded. "Please show yourself."

A young man promptly stepped out from among the trees. Staring at me pointedly, he asked, "Do you not know where you are? Are you a stranger to this place?" His piercing gaze was unnerving, but then he suddenly smiled, saying, "I know you. You live on the other side of the mountain, don't you?" It was as though a lightning bolt had struck me, and my memory immediately returned.

It was 30,000 B.C. and my name was Devnia. I was a brilliant scientist, musician and astrologer, and was a professor at the university in Atlantis. My research team was busy working on a project that enabled us to lift things by using sound. My experiences today with the fruit detaching itself just because I wanted it to intrigued me, and I was excited to test the potential of simultaneously using sound and giving mental direction in my laboratory. After chatting for a little while, we said our goodbyes and I hastened to my lab. Although it was already early evening, in Atlantis the sun rises at about five a.m. and only sets after 10 p.m. because the air is healthy and unpolluted. As such, disease was almost unheard of, no one suffered from fatigue and citizens achieved a lot on any given day.

Our latest research experiment had been resoundingly successful—we had managed to lift a house and carry it through the air using the sound of our many voices. We had discovered that as we lowered our voices, so the building slowly descended. Similarly, if the pitch of our voices became higher, objects would go up. Now, I wanted to try to actively direct objects using mind power and sound.

Perhaps a bit ambitiously, I instructed the group that our next experiment would involve lifting a huge statue and moving it to another country. The city officials had become interested in our research and had requested our help with this.

"Why do you want to carry this statue to another country?" I asked them.

"We want to rule there," they answered. "This is not the only land there is to cultivate. We have been inspecting this other country for many years. It is connected with the constellations and people from other planets. We feel we can do more there than those gods who came from the stars," they elaborated.

"This statue is a likeness of the man who ruled us before a spell was cast over him, which transformed him into having the body of a lion. Can the statue be transported to this land using your technology?" they asked.

"There is no harm in trying," I said. "Tomorrow we shall gather here at the laboratory and begin this project. Remember to meditate tonight so that you are filled with power and energy," I added.

"This man terrorized his people," my assistant told me. "He had the strength of a lion and he ruled with an iron fist, which is why the curse manifested itself with his having the mane and body of a lion but the face of a man. Ever since he was turned into a statue, our land has enjoyed much peace and we have developed tremendously without interference," she explained.

The following day, all the scientists gathered together. We sat cross-legged around this statue and began to hum. It began to move slightly, then suddenly levitated off the ground. We felt ourselves rising into the air alongside it. We focused our mental energies to direct the statue to where it should be placed. "Here we are," I said. "The statue must be put here, under the constellation of Leo." The statue slowly descended, embedding itself into the rich and fertile dark soil. "We shall return to cultivate this land and claim it for our own," one of the elders said. With that, we flew back to Atlantis, satisfied with our accomplishment.

Things were beautiful in those days. We lived in a land of plenty. God, the Ancient of Times, ruled over all the galaxies, constellations and planets, and communicated daily with our king and leader.

The Ancient of Times was beautiful, powerful and perfect in His wisdom. When he made Lucifer, tambourine and pipe music filled the air, and wherever he went, beautiful music played. Lucifer resided in Eden with God before coming to Atlantis, where he was covered from head to foot in precious stones—carnelian, topaz, diamond, beryl, onyx, jasper, sapphire, turquoise, emerald and gold. He was a sight to behold, and his beautiful wings would cover his throne.

Lucifer changed suddenly—I don't know why. I heard him say, "I want to put my throne above that of the Ancient of Times' one. I am tired of going back and forth to worship. I want to be the Almighty."

He called us together and addressed us in this way: "Who chooses to be my followers? All who do must stand on my right side; all who do not, stand on my left." I could not believe what I was hearing!

He then went on to say, "I am about to topple the throne of the Most High. Then I, Lucifer, will become the Most High. Come, my workers. Accompany me and we will declare war."

Ominously, he continued, "Those who side with me will live and those who do not will be wiped from the Earth. Their bodies will be taken and thrown out of Atlantis for the birds of the air to devour."

I feared the Ancient of Times but, at the same time knew that if I sided with Lucifer, I would be destroyed for all eternity. It took courage, but I decided to accept my fate and stood on the left side of Lucifer along with many others. Our king sadly sided with Lucifer.

"I am on my way to the throne room of the Ancient of Times to declare war," Lucifer announced. "Michael and his angels will never defeat me. When I return, I will kill you traitors. Actually, better yet, my soldiers will kill you all now!" With that he lifted up his hand and shouted, "Attack the traitors!" Within seconds I felt the sharp pain of a dagger plunging into my heart. As I lay on the ground, I knew my days in Atlantis had ended. Shortly, I felt myself floating upwards beyond the horizon. I looked around and saw the constellations; the stars made me feel as though I was in fairy land.

I sat with the Ancient of Times and watched the war that was taking place in heaven. Archangel Michael and his army battled against Lucifer and his angels and, after what seemed like hours, Lucifer and his army were defeated. The Ancient of Times threw Lucifer's soldiers out of heaven, forbidding any of them from ever returning. I watched their faces as they passed me. Some shouted their outrage and others were penitent. Lucifer was terrifying to behold—his once-beautiful face had been destroyed, his features disfigured by anger.

As I looked toward the Earth and Atlantis, I was horrified at what I saw: the entire Earth was submerged by water and had been plunged into darkness. An absolute silence reigned. Then, a majestic, booming voice resonated through the universe. "Let the waters come together in one place so that the land will appear," the Ancient of Times commanded. The Earth convulsed and the waters receded. Then he called our king to appear before him and said, "Seeing the first statue was destroyed him and said, "Seeing the first statue was destroyed.

He was returned to Atlantis and, in the centuries to come, our king got given a new name, Abdul-Hol (which means God of the East), because his stone form was located under the constellation of Leo. Nowadays, we refer to him as 'The Sphinx'.

One day, as Abdul-Hol stared into the distance, he heard the roaring and grunting of a lioness nearby. The Archangel Ariel, who takes the form of a lioness, was passing by, and she taunted him, telling him that he would never be as powerful as the Ancient of Times, creator of all things. He grew angry being mocked by some female, and wished that he could zap her with his huge paw, however that was impossible.

She flew around him many times, teasing him. She knew that he was helpless. This female lioness was indeed beautiful, and her wings shimmered in the desert heat. She was captivating. He wondered whether he could charm her into staying on as his companion.

Suddenly Abdul-Hol woke up, only to see that the Earth was still covered in water and darkness prevailed. "Well a man . . . a god . . . can dream, can't he?" he mused.

Many moons passed, and during this time I became acquainted with the stars and the gods of the horizon, especially with Osiris, his wife Isis and their son, Horus. After the waters had receded, the planets of Orion and Sirius exploded and the gods descended from heaven and settled on the earth.

---------------- **Chapter Two** ----------------

The Ancient of Times had made the heavens and the Earth, the seas and the land. He had flooded the Earth and had then caused the water to evaporate. The land was filled with the fine sand the sea had left behind when it dried up. Osiris called this the desert, and it surrounded our fallen king's monument that we had carried, before placing it beneath the constellation of Leo.

I realised I still had much to observe and learn in heaven before returning to Earth in another body, and this motivated me to question the gods. "Osiris, you are king of the underworld. Please tell me your story," I begged. So he did, although he only gave me a brief overview of his life.

Osiris tells his story

I am Osiris, god of the earth and vegetation. My wife is called Isis, and she is the most beautiful and powerful of all the goddesses in this land. She is truly loved by many and I have seen her rescue many children from negative spirits and darkness. Before this land was given the name of Egypt, we descended from the stars. We lived on another planet and we were sent by the masters of the constellations to settle here and build a nation of gods for the Ancient of Times.

We became comfortable in this world and thought we would never be attacked by anyone, but we were mistaken. One day, I got into a serious argument with my brother Seth, whose arrogance irritated me. "Who sent you to join me?" I asked.

"You know full well that I was sent here by the Ancient of Times, and I am under His command," Seth replied.

"Brother, you ran away from your responsibilities and refuse to control the spirits of the constellations. If you cannot carry out your own duties, how can you carry out mine?" I thundered

The argument grew very heated, and Seth struck and killed me.

Isis was devastated. She loved me dearly, and had lost her brother. She was about to give up all hope of restoring me to life when our sister arrived.

She had the power to raise people from the dead so, together, they worked on me. Nephthys poured out her restorative energy and Isis her love. They turned me over onto my back, and then Nephthys massaged my heart whilst Isis breathed thoughts of healing over my body. Finally, I started to breathe again. I opened my eyes and smiled up at Isis.

As I gazed at her, love filled my entire being and I recovered from my injuries.

After a few weeks had passed, I took my beautiful sister Isis for a walk. We stopped to catch our breaths, and I turned and looked at her, saying "Sister Isis, goddess of beauty, when I died, Aubis the god of the underworld told me to return and make you my wife". I took her in my arms and waited for an answer. "Yes!" she exclaimed. "Brother Osiris, god of the earth and vegetation, I will marry you." We soon married and had a son whom we named Horus.

Seth, Horus's uncle, was made Lord of Upper Egypt and became associated with the desert and the tombs. When he was a young boy, Horus became curious about the strained relationship between Seth and me. "Father, why do you not want to associate with your brother Seth?" he asked. I then told him about the argument we had had. "If you and your sister had not been close by, I would have been left in the underworld for all eternity," I said to Isis, who was standing next to me. This news made Horus angry; he had grown into a strong and powerful man and was chief of the warriors of the constellations and the gods. "I am going to settle this," he cried. "I will avenge the death of my father." With that he set off in search of Seth. He was filled with anger and hatred and attacked Seth when he found him. The battle went on for hours, and both parties were injured—Horus even lost the sight of his one eye.

In spite of this, Horus was made King of the Horizon. He became a powerful and responsible monarch and carried out his duties well. Horus was not only King of the Horizon, but also could help earthlings when they called on him. His powers also gave him insight into the past, present and future.

One day, looking at the great stone creature that had been transported from Atlantis, Horus decided to name it the Sphinx. He instinctively knew that the constellation of Leo and all the planets were connected to it. "Horus, the King of the Horizon, has named me the Sphinx," Abdul-Hol thought upon hearing Horus musing to himself about what to name the monolithic lion figure. "He thinks he knows all the mysteries that surround me, but he doesn't. I am the Father of Terror and the Giant of the East still, despite being trapped in stone."

Nobody realised just how much life and intelligence was within that stony body. People thought AbdulHol's spirit was no more, but we would soon find out that we were very much mistaken.

The identity of the Sphinx

Who are you, great creature of stone, mortar and sand, towering over the Egyptian desert facing east? Abdul-Hol? The Great Sphinx of Egypt also named the Father of Terror? Are you a descendant of Ham, the son of Noah? Are you the one true God?

How ethical are you, Sphinx? You never pressurise, condemn or interfere with other religions but you seem to impart godly wisdom while staring silently across the desert.

Who are you great god of the east, half man and half beast? What secrets are you guarding? Are you trying to tell us something? Who?

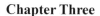

Chapter Three

D awn was breaking; the sky was streaked with red as the sun rose over the desert, revealing the great god of the east, Abdul-Hol (the Sphinx).

Many have tried to guess the age of this giant rock structure. Archaeologists estimate that it dates back to 2494 B.C., but of course this is only guesswork. Despite sophisticated computer programming and analysis, the age of the Sphinx remains a mystery. Some think that the harsh desert sands have damaged the Sphinx to the point where accurately dating its formation is impossible. Will its true age ever be scientifically proven? Let us consider the desert: miles and miles of fine sand. The biblical story of creation accounts for its formation. In Genesis, chapter one, verse one, we read of Baresheth (the dateless past) and of how God created the heavens and the Earth. Verse two describes how the Earth was without form and was void of life—how darkness reigned and the Spirit hovered over its waters.

Genesis (chapter one, verses nine to ten) reads: "Then let the waters beneath the sky be gathered into oceans so that dry land will emerge . . . [verse eleven] and so it was. God named the dry land earth and the waters seas. And God was pleased." Here is a question which needs much debate and speculation: how did the desert originate?

The bible answers this question. After the flood (Genesis, chapter one, verse six), God formed the sky and dry land. At that time the oceans still covered what is now Egypt and, over thousands of years, the waters receded, resulting in dry land and the Red Sea.

If one compares the texture of the desert sand with sea sand, one sees that there is a distinct similarity. It is no coincidence that camels traversing the desert are called 'ships of the desert'.

Archaeologists suspect the Sphinx was originally situated near the land of the Caananites, although Canaan is quite a distance from Egypt. Canaan was where Jacob (Israel) resided with his family before the great famine, and they were compelled to travel to Egypt to purchase grain.

Archeologists have come up with a theory concerning the corrosion of the Sphinx's head, and think it must be due to a flood. If that was the case, the depth of the water would have been over 20 metres! Plus, the Mortuary Temple at the base of the pyramids would also have suffered water damage . . . yet it bears no signs of this. Why would the pyramids remain undamaged by the flood but not the Sphinx? Could a tsunami really have disfigured the Sphinx? Some scientists believe that heavy rains fell in about 2500 B.C., but cannot empirically prove this.

It is obvious the Sphinx's origin is shrouded in mystery, and there are many legends and superstitions attached to it. It is a masterpiece—a work of art—that has yet to reveal its secrets.

An archaeologist called John West (along with many others) believes that the civilization responsible for building the Sphinx and its neighbouring pyramids ceased to exist long before 7000-5000 B.C. So, this would rule out the Hebrews building these pyramids.

Thoughts and private dialogue with the Sphinx

Why must I disclose my secrets to you human beings? You are creatures of destruction—always questioning, always searching for knowledge that should never be disclosed or shared. You are never ever satisfied with what you have. I, the Sphinx, will always have unspoken thoughts and deep and hidden secrets that only the God of the Universe knows. Only in His time will He reveal truths to the right people, who will cherish and not destroy with this knowledge.

I have had forensic experts and archaeologists trying to work out who I really am. Some think I was built for Khafre, a Pharaoh, but have no real proof to support such an idea.

Abdul-Hol, Father of Terror, are you carrying the secrets of the pyramids? And are you connected with the Egyptian gods? If you could, would you speak to me and tell me? Would you confide in me and teach me how to obtain power like yours?

> *I, Abdul-Hol, Father of Terror, am king of the desert. I rule with strength, power and authority. I will bring down and destroy any enemies.*
>
> *Why all these questions, human of the south? Listen a while and I will tell you about when Moses led the people past me to the Red Sea while fleeing Egypt and its cruel taskmasters. But first, I must relate many other incidents that transpired here before he left Egypt. I, Abdul-Hol, was an eye-witness to all these things.*

Egypt, you were a chosen land destined for many of God's miracles. How many strange gods from the skies inhabited you before you had a name, and what miraculous healings and strange inventions your people came up with. It doesn't seem all that strange that life forms on other planets would mimic your Sphinx, as seen on Mars by astronauts while orbiting the Earth.

Sphinx, are you an image of an ascended master? Can one experience holistic healing by meditating upon your image: half man and half beast? Reveal to me the truth of your being; reveal to me the secret of your power, the power you brought with you when you descended from the stars, mystical giant of the east.

The Scriptures speak of the cornerstone being Jesus and that we are living stones that are part of a structure that points upward. Where are we in this Spiritual Pyramid? Are we in the foundation, in the middle, or near the top? Are we reaching for the sky? Do we belong to Orion or are we earthbound? Are we connected to the Sphinx? Were we always Earth beings? Did we come from another planet? Does the Sphinx hold the answers to these questions?

What an exciting thought to explore the worlds unknown and to discover who we really are: earthlings or star people.

Chapter Four

It is a fact that stones have been split by using the sound of voices at a certain pitch. Was this the method used to cut the giant stones of the pyramids and is that how they were made? Were the pyramids lifted from their home (perhaps on Mars) and carried through the air and placed where they now stand?

Did creatures from another planet deposit the pyramids and, after fulfilling their mission, return to their home planet? Can you answer me, Abdul-Hol, Father of Terror, God of the East, who was worshipped and still is by many who believe you are part deity?

In the Scriptures we read that Jesus said: "If you had faith the size of a mustard seed, you can say to the mountain 'Be thou cast into the sea' and it shall be done." Bearing that in mind, how can we doubt that the people responsible for this wonder of the world may have used their faith to transport the Sphinx. It is not only our generation that believes in a Higher Power. People have always believed in a supreme being.

In Genesis (chapter six, verse two) we read about heavenly beings who married beautiful women, resulting in the women giving birth to giants. How can we prove beings from other planets have not done a similar thing when visiting Earth? They may even have been responsible for the creation of the Sphinx. It could even be possible that sphinxes exist on many other planets.

Jesus told the multitudes that God could even make the stones rise up to worship Him. Whether stones or people, we are all composed of matter that makes us 'alive' (whether an inanimate rock or a breathing human being). The breath of God, the very same breath that fills our lungs, gives 'life' to the materials the Sphinx is composed of.

It is not just our faith that can move mountains though. The mountains are capable of responding to our faith, because the mountain can 'hear' and 'feel' your God-invested power and responds accordingly.

The Sphinx answers

I remember, child of the earth, the day Moses passed me by with a great multitude. They were unruly and grumbling. I can see for many miles and when I looked across the desert, I watched Moses drawing near to the Red Sea. I suddenly became aware of the Egyptian army following them. It became clear to me they were intending to force Moses and his people to return to Egypt. I then noticed the sky become dark as a cloud covered them. The soldiers found it difficult to follow as the cloud made it difficult to see clearly.

Suddenly a strong wind began to blow, and it blew in a way that I thought was strange. It seemed to occur mainly over the Red Sea. I became more curious than ever and contacted the constellations to ask what was happening. "The Red Sea is opening and the Great Spirit of the Universe has made a path for the Hebrews to walk across dry land," they answered. I was excited at the news and asked Leo to keep me informed.

After what seemed like a full day, Leo told me that the Egyptians were making an effort to cross over to the other side of the sea and that the wheels of their chariots were falling off. All the soldiers drowned and as their spirits passed me on their way back to Egypt, I could hear them telling each other that this disaster was undoubtedly at the hand of God. It was. He stopped them from capturing the Hebrews. "We all drowned, accomplishing nothing," they complained. "We did not believe Moses and respect the mighty power he displayed before Pharaoh when he performed miracles. Now we are doomed to the underworld of darkness, and who knows for how long?"

I, the Sphinx, ask this question: "Did they not know they could not fight against the Higher Power I have heard some call the Ancient of Times and others God, especially after all the miracles Moses demonstrated to the Pharaoh?"

The sand storm

The sun was at its zenith when the Sphinx suddenly heard a rumbling sound. He looked across the desert and noticed dust rising. "Oh my!" he exclaimed. "A sand storm is brewing; I had better close my eyes. I sincerely hope I am not completely covered with sand as I have been many times before. It looks as though this sand storm will be a severe one." The Sphinx had hardly uttered these words before the storm struck.

The desert sands piled higher and higher, first covering the Mortuary Temple, then the front paws of the Sphinx. The sand was now up to its mouth, and the storm showed no signs of abating. The fierce winds howled incessantly.

"Oh, my eyes; they are covered with sand," the Sphinx cried. "Only the top of my head is still visible to the world. I hope the wind changes direction to blow the sand off my face!" As if by some miracle, that is exactly what happened.

The Great Sphinx, the god of the desert, has become one of the wonders of the world and is connected to the gods of the Nile. Beneath it are passages; some are concealed and some have been worn away by flood waters.

Over the centuries, it has kept many of the gods' secrets, but now the gods are revealing their secrets to a select few who believe in the ancients.

One day, the Sphinx saw a star larger than any he had ever seen before. The spirits told him it was a sign that a great king was about to be born. He heard the sound of many bells ringing in the distance. "Where does this music come from, I wonder," he mused. Then the sound of voices drew closer and closer. He saw Magi making their way across the desert. They spoke about a king and how they were following his star, which was directly over Bethlehem in Israel.

The Sphinx realised that the sound of bells came from the ornaments tied around the camels' necks. The bells and voices became louder and louder as these men travelled with their desert ships. Their excitement was palpable.

"Who is this Great King whose sign is in the stars?" he wondered. "He must be very important to have a star above his birthplace."

The Sphinx watched hundreds of men travel eastward in search of this king. The procession seemed to go on for hours, and he listened to their animated discussions about Bethlehem as they passed, casting silhouettes against his stone body in the moonlight.

The desert grew silent once again, disturbed only by the occasional sounds of a desert creature scuttling in the sands.

I can hear many voices drifting on the wind, women crying, children screaming. What is happening?" the Sphinx asked the gods.

"It is a prophecy being fulfilled. After the Magi visited Herod, he ordered that all male children below the age of two be killed. He is angry and jealous and does not welcome the idea of another king. The Magi were warned by an angel and returned to their homes travelling in the opposite direction from where they came. The Magi did not tell Herod where to find this newborn king, and this made him angry; he refuses to give up his throne."

The sun was already hot and it beat down mercilessly as the Sphinx gazed across the desert.

Suddenly he saw movement. "What is that?" he cried. "Ah, it is a man walking with his donkey which is carrying a woman and a young child." Next to them was an angel who had instructed them to go to Egypt until God told them it would be safe to return to Israel. "Who are these people?" the Sphinx asked the angel. "It is Joseph, Mary and Jesus, whom God instructed to go to Egypt because Herod wishes to kill the young child Jesus." He mulled on this for some time, acknowledging that this child must be very special.

A few years passed before the Sphinx saw them returning to Israel. "Why are they returning?" he asked the angel that was accompanying them. "God instructed them to return because Herod is now dead," the angel replied.

The Sphinx kept tabs on the child Jesus, and received regular reports from the angels and the constellations about how he was growing into a strong and powerful man who could perform miracles. One day, the angels told him that Jesus had been crucified. Gazing toward Jerusalem, he saw clouds gathering. A voice that sounded like thunder was then carried to him by the desert wind: "Why do you gaze in such wonder toward heaven? You see Jesus going up into the clouds to heaven and are saddened, but I tell you that he will return."

The Sphinx knew that Jesus had ascended to His kingdom in a cloud; that he was the Prince of Peace and the Son of God.

The Sphinx had heard and seen many things, but none so astonishing as the events surrounding the life and death of Jesus. He had heard voices carried by the desert winds and had conjured visions of humankind's future. His conversations with the stars and angels made him realise just how connected the constellations were to the fate of earthlings. He absorbs their energy and draws strength from the sun, which infuses him with healing power. Sadly, not many humans know that the Sphinx has miraculous healing potential.

Because the Sphinx's spiritual eye is open, he can see departed spirits in the netherworld, some surrounded by darkness and others by light. He has seen spirit beings with wings; these winged creatures fly to and fro, filling the air with music as they play their harps and sing praises to the Most High God of the Universe. Some beings fly so high they reach the constellation of Leo, after which they return with renewed energy and insight. They encircle the Sphinx and impart some of their energy to him, allowing him to see and hear a great many things that human eyes and ears cannot register. This Great Giant and god of the desert will reveal deep secrets to those who seek the truth for altruistic purposes.

Chapter Six

The Sphinx observed how the number of Egypt's gods increased, each taking on the tasks allocated by Horus of the Horizon. The stars are connected even though many gods are earthbound spirits and are called Ascended Masters. They have immense power and may work with heavenly beings to help earthlings (particularly children) achieve their goals.

The Sphinx saw how children were in danger. "Isis, wife of Osiris and lover of children, help these little ones," he implored. "Show them how to deal with their troubles, and protect them from the darkness and dangers that are waiting to hurt them, or even kill them." His prayer was answered when Isis suddenly arrived in a royal chariot. This beautiful, powerful goddess rescued the little children from imminent danger.

Many moons have passed, and religions and fashions have changed. The Sphinx witnessed a man named Sai-ed-Dahr climb up to his face and damage his nose. No one has repaired it, and the gods, angry at his actions, covered the whole of Giza with sand. Today, it forms part of the desert.

Anyone who tries to destroy the Sphinx will be cursed by the gods. However, the gods are good-natured and, just as the Sphinx can call upon them for assistance, children of the earth can also do so. With the gods' help, their troubles will vanish as though the winds of the desert have blown them away.

---------------- **Chapter Seven** ----------------

The Great Giant of the desert knows your desires will be fulfilled, so you should always have faith that your wishes will be met. The Scriptures prove that the miraculous is not far-fetched: Moses' rod turned into a serpent; the rivers and waters of the Nile turned into blood; and a plague of frogs invaded Egypt. The Sphinx has seen all of these things come to pass.

The Sphinx explains

The hand of the great and mighty God of the Universe poured out His anger on the children of the Earth. Learn from it: turn away from the dark path which you are walking and tread no longer through the thorny bushes of sin; bump your feet no more on the stony sidewalks. Decide to walk straight on the narrow path, and the angels will protect you as they protect me. Children of the earth, listen to the message I am sending you. Change your thinking, then your ways and attitude and you can be sure your life will change. I, the Great Sphinx, the God of the Desert, the Father of Terror, have spoken; take my advice and live.

Whose eyes glow in the dark, observing the creatures of the desert? Whose thoughts fill the atmosphere, day and night? Whose power do we feel as we pass the pyramids?

All you are asking has but one answer . . . me. The spirits in the pyramids are subject to my power because I am connected to three worlds: the constellations, the earth, and the underworld. I have much knowledge of these worlds and a magnetic drawing power. Even the sun is led by me and rises as my moods change. My countenance changes at different times of the day and during different seasons. As the shadows of the evening cover my face, so my expression changes to being peaceful beyond description. In winter my spirit is low as the nights are cold; in summer I feel more comfortable. People think I am an inanimate object, but you now know better. I am made from the same substance you are. I react to vibrations and I am formed from minerals, atoms and molecules—just like you are. We were both made from dust. When I hear earthlings criticise me, my emotions run low; on days when I am admired, my emotions run high. That is the reason I, the Sphinx, can understand you children of the earth. If I should be broken down, I will return to dust, just as you will when you leave your earthly body. We have the same universal god and we must worship daily. This is the message I, the Great Giant of the Desert, the great and mighty Sphinx, the Father of Terror, am giving you.

And so it is . . .

Suddenly I saw myself in my mother's arms, wrapped in a pink blanket. I watched myself growing into the person I am today—it was like watching a movie of my life's important moments. I awoke when my husband opened the front door.

"Hello, my darling. Yes, thank you; it was a most unusual day. I will tell you all about it over a cup of tea."

After I had finished relating the adventures I experienced while meditating, my husband said, "This is amazing and, what is more, I believe you regressed. I believe every word. I also do not believe it was a dream."

FROM THE
BEGINNING
OF TIME

---**CHAPTER ONE**---

HOW IT ALL BEGAN

N O PAST; NO PRESENT; NO FUTURE; JUST AN EMPTY SPACE!! A form that resembled a man appeared His beard was white and long, reaching down to His waist as He who stood; there appeared like crystalline brightness of Jasper and the fiery sardius. And encircling Him was a halo that looked like a rainbow of emerald. A few minutes later, a second form appeared His hair was white like wool, as white as snow; His eyes flashed like a flame of fire; His feet like burnished bright bronze as it was refined in a furnace; His voice was like the sound of many waters as He greeted the One who first appeared." We are Gods who have come to create a new galaxy", the first God said. As He spoke, both Gods raised their hands, out of which came flashes of lightning, their voices sounded like thunder, and echoed for many miles into the empty space. Immediately, a beautiful garden appeared trees with fruit, flowers, green vegetable leaves, appeared great preparation was being made for the future.

The next to appear was a beautiful palace made from the rarest Ivory, the floor was made from marble, around the thrones were seven gold pillars. The palace had many rooms, of which one was filled with stardust. There were streets of purest gold. Within the Ivory walls precious stones of every kind were imbedded, adding to the radiant light that shone from the Spirits of the Ancient of Times and the second God.

The Gods spoke in a strange tongue that only they could understand, spongy seeds appeared on the branches of the trees, the Gods began to blow on them and as they did, the seeds fell to the ground that had been formed in the garden, and began to grow, "You shall be called Angels," we were told by the Gods "and you will have wings and will be able to fly wherever we send you and do our bidding." The most wonderful thing that happened, we discovered we could all communicate telepathically, we were celestial beings. This did not bother us as we were informed that we were not angels alone, but spirit beings, power was given to us. Instinctively we knew the Gods who created us had to be worshipped. The Archangels who had been created before us stood around the throne on which the Ancient of Times who had first arrived sat. They lifted their voices in worship, we joined them. This was a wonderful experience I never forgot.

These angelic beings communicated with the two Gods in what is now known as the tongues of angels.

We were instructed to enter the stardust chamber and fill large containers with the dust, after which we were told to fly out into space and empty them, this we did, the stars were formed and given their place, each one was given a name. We returned to the heavenly palace with great happiness knowing our mission was successful. The stars discovered they could sing, they lifted their voices in praise to their creator, the louder they sang the more they shone. The next to be created were the sun and moon. The Two Gods decided the space around these two great heavenly elements needed to be filled. Once again they lifted their arms and spoke in their strange language, there was an explosion; planets began to form and take their places around the sun. They rotated on their own axis, gradually moving around the sun. We now know it takes three hundred and sixty five and a quarter days to complete that journey.

As time went by, thousands upon thousands of angels were created, a similar way the stars and star people came into being.

Elementals were created; they were humanoids who lived on various planets, occasionally visiting the celestial palace to obtain seeds to plant on the planets of their choice.

Osiris along with his wife Isis and son Horus were gods, they too visited the celestial palace and were given seeds and shrubs from the celestial garden to cultivate on planet Earth at that time was not yet given the name Atlantis. He was made the god of the vegetation, images of his self and Isis were built, and later of his son Horus, who became acquainted with the Gods that were later to stay in a section of the planet that has not yet been called Egypt. And so, this is how the Spirit world increased.

Lucifer the most beautiful Archangel had musical instruments built within his entire body. He was adorned with all kinds of precious jewels, as he walked music came from his body, the precious jewels shone and gave off the most beautiful rainbow lights, the angels were enchanted by his beauty, he walked on the Holy mountain with the Ancient of Times, and was told he would be given a world of his own to rule. The Ancient of Times; gave him a palace, a throne and a crown, he put the power of the Spirit upon him and made him a prophet. He was given a sanctuary, this made him a priest, he was given knowledge this made him a PROPHET, PRIEST AND KING. He was told he could take angels of his choice to planet earth and set up his kingdom. After his ordination, he was sent to planet earth along with his angels.

After they departed, all the celestial beings were summoned to the great hall in the palace. Even though we were angels, we were given the choice to remain angels or become incarnate angels and be sent to live in the kingdom of Lucifer as humans. We were promised that we would not lose our angelic powers, any time we desired, we could fly to any planet to visit, we would be given the ability to open and shut doors and gates without touching them and do many wonderful things, Spiritual gifts would be unlimited, but, we had to make a covenant with God, we had to serve Him and reverence Him forever and not follow any other God. These conditions pleased many angels of which a very special angel and I were a part. We chose to still carry the name of God within us. With that my friend was named Elshady which was taken from the Almighty's attribute THE ALL SUFFICIENT ONE. (EL SHEDDAI) I was given the name Elshalomia, The God of peace (EL SHALOM). The moment had arrived for us to leave our celestial home and move to planet earth. On our way to earth, we decided to fly among the stars, "Look, we are passing Gemini, these twins are unpredictable, try never to upset them, we will soon pass Taurus, and he is strong and fierce." Just then, an angel pointed and said; "There is Libra, at times unbalanced, we must not forget Leo, he is the king of the constellations, strong and domineering, he likes to be noticed.

Lucifer asked the Ancient of Days whether he could change the name of earth to something else. You may not change the name of the planet, but the name of the land on which I have set up your city, from THE LAND THAT IS, to ATLANTIS. This new name pleased Lucifer.

Tyre was a suburb of Atlantis, Lucifer made one of the incarnated angels king. He communicated with the star gods, some were good and some fierce, they made war against Lucifer who defeated them.

The inhabitants of the planets which had not yet been named and some of which were unknown made war against Lucifer, there were many fierce battles, Lucifer over powered the enemy and won. The gods of these planets fought to take over planet earth, but this was not allowed at that time by the Ancient of Days.

Aliens by the thousands arrived on planet Earth in their spacecrafts, some were humanoids and others weirdly shaped creatures. Many were dark skinned with dark brown eyes and others blonde and had blue eyes, others with auburn hair and green eyes. Each type came from a different planet, or star.

CHAPTER TWO

THE INVASION

I discovered I was a brilliant scientist, astrologer and musician, along with my fellow incarnate angels, we could levitate any object with the power of our minds and at times with a humming sound, I began to enjoy being a human, with powers such as these, we had no right to complain.

An evil creature arrived from a planet unknown to any of us, he had the face of a man and mane and body of a lion, along with him other creatures that had faces of animals and bodies of humans arrived, they were determined to over power Lucifer and take over Atlantis, this battle soon came to an end, Lucifer and his angels fought and won the war they drove out many of these creatures, but, no matter how hard they tried, they could not get rid of this lion man who was determined to disrupt the earth and take away Lucifer's power.

One of the incarnate angels chose to become a wizard and could cast spells, turned this lion man into stone, we were all amazed to see this, and were grateful, but now, what do we do with this monster? He took up so much space, the town clerk Lucifer chose to see to these matters called a meeting, all the scientists and astrologers had to attend, two hundred were chosen, we were informed that we were to transport this lion man to one of Osiris' gardens and leave him there under the constellation of Leo.

The following morning, we were given our places, we surrounded this lion man, began to meditate, and simultaneously began to make a humming sound, this great object of stone began to levitate and float to where it was directed our journey seemed never to end, at last we reached our destination, slowly this lion man was lowered and finally was settled on the ground. "Now what should we name this great stone object?" we asked our leader the wizard who put the spell on this great monster, "Because he is made into rock and stone, we shall name him the SPHINX"

"EXCELLENT!!" We shouted. "At last we have got rid of this monster" "And he will be here for as long as the gods of the planets allow;" said the wizard.

We no sooner got rid of the Sphinx when there was a rumbling sound in the distance, it grew steadily louder, the Draconian Reptilians appeared they came from the Draco Star System, we discovered they were cunning and intelligent and warlike creatures their skins were dark greenish and grey and their eyes were reptile like, their feet were webbed. Atlantis once again lost its peaceful atmosphere with the arrival of these aliens; "What is becoming of this place?" I asked my friend "I do not know," she replied, "but what ever it is, I do not like it," Once again, the warriors went into battle, and they drove out these creatures. "It is in times such as these," I wistfully said, "I regret coming to live on planet earth, when we lived with the Ancient of times, we lived in peace," "I agree with what you are saying;" my friend replied.

Creatures from unknown planets arrived, they informed us they were gods and were given duties to perform on planet earth. "What kind of duties?" Our leader enquired. "To help with the underworld and vegetation," they replied. "That is the duty Osiris was given, I do not think you are being honest," our leader exclaimed. "You can ask the Ancient of times if you are in doubt, as you see, Planet Earth is becoming populated with all kinds of strange creatures and Osiris needs help." "I see;" our leader replied, "very well then, I will show you where you may build yourselves a place of shelter." "Thank you," they replied.

CHAPTER THREE

THE PLEIADIANS

A new day dawned, planet Earth was about to receive visitors, our leader had received a message from the Pleiades, we were informed they were coming in peace and if they were impressed with what they saw, they would ask permission to remain here for a season, but intended to return to their home after they had learned enough about our customs. After much thought and discussion with the board, they voted unanimously. The Pleidians arrived and taught us much about themselves. They too communicated telepathically

"Welcome to our planet Earth" Lucifer greeted the leader of the Pleideans, "Thank you," was the response "From which planet have you come?" enquired Lucifer. "We are located in the constellation of Taurus the Bull, tonight you will notice a small cluster of seven stars they are five hundred light years from here each star in the Pleiades system has a name would you like me to tell you what they are?" "Yes please" Lucifer answered with a touch of excitement,

he was always eager to learn something new. "Well"
the leader began, noticing a crowd of curious
spectators gathering. "We get Taygeta, second Maya,
third Coela fourth, Atlas fifth Merope, sixth Electra,
seventh Alcoyne. Because of the many wars on Lyra,
many peaceful Lyrans left on their spacecrafts and
travelled for many years till they came upon the seven
cluster stars on the Pleiades. The inhabitants there
are humanoids as we are; King Horus of the Horizon
gave them permission to visit Earth whenever it suited
them." "That is wonderful!" Lucifer exclaimed waving
his arms and giving a little jump.

Thousands of years passed and the heavens were
filled with stars. Many light years beyond the stars that
were invisible to the humans on Earth, planets and
stars were created, there was more than one Galaxy,
the angels Lucifer sent out to see how the world was
progressing returned with this information.

The El hyhybrids arrived from a distant
planet many light years from planet Earth, they
were creatures of super human and strength and
intelligence and abilities, they were often thought to
be the first people on planet Earth, they had similar
powers to Cronus the Universal god and Rhea who are
the parents of Zeus the Greek god. These gods felt it
necessary to come to planet Earth, as the gods of the
other planets wanted to rule them.

The sky became dark, we were about to be invaded
by the Neonates. Lucifer commanded his guards
to sound the trumpets to summon his warriors to
war, they arrived with shining swords and shields,
spears and daggers, lined up and awaited Lucifer's
command.

They fought fiercely that day, many of the Neonates escaped on their spacecraft when they realized they were losing the battle, some were either taken prisoner or killed. The Orions heard about the war between the Neonates and Lucifer and decided to free the Neonates from their prison in which they were placed, but they knew they were not strong enough to do it alone, they called upon the Zeta Riticuli systems to join forces, this they did and returned to planet Earth to over power Lucifer and his warriors, but they lost the battle.

With each victory, Lucifer became more and more proud, "I have not only beauty but power!" he exclaimed throwing his head back and raising his sword. "I am going to declare war, the gods of the stars and planets will know I am a god, and soon will be the god of the entire creation. I will conquer wherever I go." All these happenings took place millions of years before Lucifer took the courage to go against the Ancient of Times.

CHAPTER FOUR

THE PYRAMIDS

O sisris built two large structures out of a special stone he brought from his home planet, these structures had a wide base and their points pierced the blue sky, they towered over the Sphinx. There were passages and many rooms and a special area where Anubis the Jackal-god of the mummification was to reside.

On the completion of these structures, Osiris decided to place them along side the Sphinx. These structures had to be given a name, he asked a friend of his named Pyra, medes, Osiris decided to name these structures in honour of his friend, "I think Pyramids will be a good name to call them," Osiris said. This pleased his friend.

"This calls for a celebration, let us invite the gods of the planets, he sent out invitations, which were gladly accepted.

The day of the celebration dawned, the gods arrived in ivory chariots drawn by unicorns, they parked in the place prepared for such an occasion. The feasting lasted three days, everyone in Atlantis was invited, the last night of the feast was full moon, the spirits of the aliens who were defeated and killed by Lucifer and his warriors were summoned and given a place to rest in the underworld, and Anubis was initiated and from that moment, became the god of the underworld, part of which was under the Pyramids and the Sphinx.

After the feasts, Lucifer fought against the gods of the planets, this battle was different from the others, he wanted to possess their planet, and he wanted to reign. Pride and greed filled his heart, no longer was he satisfied with what he had. The time had come to face the Ancient of Times, even if he had to go to war with Michael the chief warring angel whose power was incomparable; it would be worth the effort.

CHAPTER FIVE

LUCIFER REBELS

Lucifer called a board meeting, he had been behaving in a strange manner, and we sensed things were about to change. The town clerk sounded the alarm which summoned everyone to the town square, Lucifer's warriors stood to attention as the people filed in. "Something is very wrong," Elshady said "I also have that feeling," Elshalomia said.

One of the board members befriended my friend and I and fed us information; in turn we told the Peiladians all we heard. "Lucifer is preparing to over throw the Ancient of Times; we had better prepare ourselves for trouble." Elshady told their leader. "I will warn my people, they must prepare themselves to leave at a moment's notice." with that he sent a telepathic message to all the Peiladians. Within minutes, objects floated past us and entered the spacecraft. That evening, not one Peiladian remained in Atlantis.

"Why have the Peiladians left?" Lucifer asked "They had everything they desired during their stay;

there was not even a farewell." He became angry, "Someone had betrayed my confidence, and there is a spy in our midst. When I find the culprit, he or she will surely die." This made Lucifer more determined to fight against The Ancient of Times. War was declared, all who were on Lucifer's side had to move to the left of the square, and all who sided with the Ancient of Times on the right. Death hung over the followers of the Ancient of Times; the soldiers were commanded to kill everyone who did not side with Lucifer. My friend and I along with hundreds of others felt a sharp pain as a spear pierced our hearts; we fell to the ground and breathed our last. Our spirits floated up toward the stars. My friend and I held hands, higher and higher we floated, until we arrived at the palace, many of the others arrived there before us. All the deceased were shown to a large hall, it was a de ja vu experience. There we awaited the outcome of the rebellion. Lucifer arrived in all his pomp his followers close behind; this was something to behold.

The Ancient of Times gave him an audience. "What is your request?" Lucifer was asked. "I have come to take the kingdom out of your hands and will lift my throne above yours, YOU! Ancient of Times will be subject to me, I have won all the battles from the beginning of time and I will win this one." The Ancient of Times, lifted his hand and beckoned to Archangel Michael to come forward, this he did followed by his warriors, they were expecting this for sometime and were prepared, they spent days praying and worshipping the Great Master the Ancient of Times and the result of this was power and strength. "We will fight for this, no one can stop me now, I will become the HEAD OF ALL THE UNIVERSE." With that he raised his sword and took a step toward Archangel Michael. The battle had begun, it continued for days, till at last, Lucifer and his followers were thrown out of the palace into the space between the third heaven and Atantis.

The two Gods lifted their hands, spoke in an unknown tongue, there was an explosion and the entire Earth was covered in water. A new dispensation was about to begin.

CHAPTER SIX

THE NEW DISPENSATION

The Ancient of Times spoke and the water receded, the Sphinx and the two pyramids were still in tact. The beautiful garden of Osiris was no more, new seeds were planted in his garden but not around the Sphinx as before, the land had become a desert. The sand was no longer rich and dark, as the waters dried it became as fine as sea sand. This is a sign that the sea covered the Sphinx and the two pyramids. No longer did the points thereof reach the blue sky and tower over the Sphinx, the sand had become soft and the pyramids sank a few feet as the waters receded as far as the Red sea. This made the Sphinx feel superior to them. The spirits and people of the future will notice him first. Pride filled the heart of the Sphinx, he was about to become the Great Giant of the Desert. Osiris often visited the Sphinx and they communicated telepathically it was on one of those occasions that Osiris gave him the name of ABDUL-HOL. The gods of the planets and constellations gave him the name of the fierce one.

Many gods feared him, there had been times they desired to visit him when fierce vibrations flowed from him, this deterred them, resulting in the Sphinx to live a very lonely life. The gods decided to call the sandy land a DESERT because the land had become deserted. All the humans had been either killed by Lucifer's army or drowned by the flood.

Whilst all this took place on planet Earth, (let us look at the parenthesis)

In the conference room of the Celestial Palace, the Ancient of Times and the other God who was second to make an appearance at the beginning of time, sat down with the Spirit who manifested all things they discussed the future of Planet Earth. "The Ancient of Times was the first to speak, "I have been thinking," He said, "We shall create humans, they will be called man, and they will be made in our Image. They will be able to create substance with the word of their mouths, and speak things into existence, their power will lay in their thoughts and the words they speak. If they remain continually in our presence, and have fellowship with us, they will have eternal life. We will plant a garden with various types of fruit, creatures of various kinds will fill the garden, this man we create can take care of this garden, we will name it Eden, it will be peaceful, and filled with our presence, the Spirit will guide them, and we will daily walk with him in the garden, the evenings will be the best time." They voted unanimously. The following day, The Ancient of Times, went to the garden, he had the blue print of this human in his mind, he drew the first man to be created in his image in the sand; built him up as one would a sand castle stood back and looked at his work, being satisfied he blew air into his nostrils; life entered him; and the creature called man arose from the dust a perfect beautiful work of art.

The Ancient of Times called this first man Adam; he tended the gardens of Eden,

Planet Earth had changed since the flood waters receded; the gods from the planets and stars came to speculate, they were pleased with what they discovered, there was plenty of land available for aliens to settle. They arrived by the thousands, bringing various species of creatures, some brought Dinosaur eggs, others creepy creatures, others brought some of their inhabitants they no longer desired to have on their planets. These had protruding jaws high cheek bones, hairy bodies, they were humanoids, their way of communicating was by making grunting sounds, they were not creatures of high intelligence but were very aggressive that was the reason they were exiled. Most of the aliens were seeking peace, they were tired of the star wars, planet Earth was the most suitable of all planets. They settled, had families and increased rapidly in number.

Millions of years passed, the gods in this time fought many battles amongst themselves, greed and jealousy being the main reason.

The inhabitants of planet Earth were becoming corrupt, the Ancient of Times became angry and decided to wipe everyone from the Earth, once again there was a meeting with the three main people of the Celestial board, they decided to send a flood, but they had a plan to save a family and pairs of creatures. They decided on a man named Noah, he was told to build an ark, take his wife and three sons and their wives aboard because they were the only eight who found favour with the Celestial board.

This news reached the ears of the Sphinx, "OH NO! NOT AGAIN, DO I HAVE TO BE COVERED WITH WATER? FOR HOW LONG THIS TIME?" He became angry with the Ancient of Times, "THIS IS GOING TOO FAR! WHY MUST WE ALL SUFFER BECAUSE OF THE DISOBEDIENT PEOPLE?" His thoughts were so loud, it reached the stars, and all the gods were distressed with this news. All they had built was once again going to be destroyed; they felt this was grossly unfair. The angels were sent to warn them not to rebel against the Ancient of Times, the gods repented and returned to their planets. Anubis was told to prepare the underworld for many spirits were about to arrive because the whole earth was going to be destroyed. This he did with the feeling of great excitement and importance. This would be the most important assignment he had ever experienced. For the first time since creation, the heavens opened and water poured forth from the clouds, the inhabitants only knew about the mist and springs in the ground watering the plants. The ark floated on the waters, after the rain stopped, many days passed, Noah and his family waited patiently for the water to reside; at last, Noah and his family and all the creatures in the ark once again walked on dry ground.

The gods were given permission to build and inhabit planet Earth, they brought many of their statues and strange creatures with them, and they set up their kingdom and called it Egypt. The Sphinx and the pyramids still stood, only now the pyramids had sunk even lower into the sand, this pleased the

Sphinx. He felt more powerful than ever. The Ancient of Times allowed the Sphinx to be once more under the constellation of Leo. Osiris, built a third pyramid it towered above the other two, it was the same height as the Sphinx, this made him angry, the animosity that was felt then still exists to this day.

Hundreds of years passed, aliens lived on planet Earth for a while; learnt all they could then returned to their own planets. They often left behind descendants; some were fierce, others gentle and peace loving. The creatures in the waters and on the earth increased in number; the humanoids from the other planets; along with the Angels and gods travelled back and forth on a daily basis, watching and reporting the actions of the inhabitants of the planet Earth to the Ancient of Times.

Gods, guides and ascended masters were ordained to help the Earthlings; they worked in conjunction with the angels.

CHAPTER SEVEN

REINCARNATION

Elshady and I were inseparable, and we loved to float among the stars, becoming acquainted with the gods of the planets. Isis often joined us; she taught us many things about her home planet. Her love for children and her gift she had to heal, especially the broken hearted; this resulted in her being called upon. "All you must do to achieve any goal; is to believe." This teaching remained alive in my heart; I did not realize at the time what an impact it would have on my future lives.

The Ancient of Times summoned all the incarnate angels who were killed by Lucifer's soldiers, we were given a choice, to remain in the Celestial realm or return to earth through a human being. Of course, we would be sent to a foreign land and given another name, some would still have their spiritual gifts and others would not. Elshady and I looked at each other, "Should we request being twins?" she asked me. "I think that would be wonderful," I replied. We were granted our request. The next thing we knew, we were in a tiny seed, slowly we felt ourselves moving down a long tunnel, it had a pinkish colour, after a few days, we found ourselves in a dark area, we were continually moving, we could hear someone speaking in a strange tongue, Elshady and I wondered what was happening to us, we felt stifled in this confined space, after being able to float around amongst the stars, now here we were cramped up, as we grew, our legs began to cramp, we kicked and moved our heads trying to become more comfortable, "When are we going to get out of this place?" I said to Elshady, "I hope soon," she responded.

One morning, we felt as though we were being squeezed into a little passage, "What is happening?" Elshady asked, "I think we are being pushed out of this place, maybe this is what happens when we must enter the world through our new mother." I said feeling breathless. Suddenly I heard screams and a voice saying, "Start panting, do not push." There was a movement that was unfamiliar to us. "I am leaving this confined space, it looks as though you are about to follow" I said. No sooner had I said this I felt myself being pulled through this narrow tunnel, Elshady followed soon afterward. "You have twin girls, they are both healthy," a man's voice said. We had become familiar with the language our new mother spoke, as we heard it daily over the past nine months we were in her womb. "I am so grateful to God for this," a woman's voice said. Elshady and I were given two smacks on the buttocks, we started to cry. "There is nothing wrong with their lungs a woman's" voice said. We were bathed and dressed in little night dresses, and placed in our new mother's arms. This was the beginning of a new life. Elshady was named Patricia and I was named Louise, we were now one year old and had taken our first step. We were both dressed in pretty pink dresses, and placed in our high chairs. Many people gathered in the room in which we sat, we had our first birthday party. Everyone brought a gift, we were very blessed.

The years passed, we were now five years of age, this was to be our fifth party, we could appreciate this; children arrived with their parents. There was a doll's house, clowns and plenty of cakes and sweets, we learned we were children of a Duchess, and we lived in a land of luxury.

The following year we were to attend school for the first time; Patricia began to cry, she was afraid to leave home all day without her nurse. The thought of school excited me; I loved to learn about new things, leaving my nurse did not bother me.

Patricia never enjoyed going to school, where I could not wait for the holidays to pass. I found school exciting, I scored high marks in every subject, where Patricia struggled, the reason for this was, and she refused to study. I on the other hand was continually doing so. Patricia became envious, "It is not fair Louise always achieves high marks," she said sulkily, "Well my dear child," our mother said, "She does study hard, and if you did the same, you too could achieve high marks;" this made Patricia even more angry.

The years sped by, we were now about to celebrate our twenty first birthday, there was much excitement as preparations were being made. We were to have a banquet after which a ball, the Royal family, and every Duke and Duchess, imaginable were invited, it was a wonderful occasion, and we were showered with gifts.

Patricia and I looked beautiful in our evening gowns and diamond tiaras, it was that night, and Patricia met her husband to be. He was a nobleman from France, they fell in love at first sight, and two months later they were married. I was too interested in studying further, music was my first love, then came science, after which I developed a strange fascination for astrology, never realizing or even remembering I had the same interests in Atlantis. My old life was completely forgotten by my natural mind, but my spirit retained the knowledge. I became a Psychic Medium, for anyone from the Royal family to be involved in such matters was a disgrace. I pretended to stop practicing these things but; secretly still continued.

Patricia's marriage was a disaster, she gave birth to a son, she named him Alfred when he was twelve, Patricia who suffered from depression, committed suicide, and she threw herself over a cliff not far from the castle in which she lived. My mother took Alfred with her to Ireland; there he lived until she passed away. I continued to study whenever I used my spiritual powers, exciting and strange things happened; this was better than getting married. I was left a considerable sum of money in my parent's estate. I never saw much of my father he was in the Royal navy and was away at sea most of my life. He died at the age of ninety, my mother at eighty five. My nephew married a Norwegian princess and moved to Norway, he became a father of three daughters and a son.

I had reached my ninetieth birthday, I had become frail, the doctors had given up hope, and I knew it was time for me to prepare to move on to another realm, this happened just before my ninety first birthday. I found myself floating amongst the stars, memories flooded back; it was wonderful to be back in the celestial realm after all this time.

Patricia and I were reunited, this was a happy occasion.

CHAPTER EIGHT

PARANORMAL

We stood before the Ancient of Times, and His Son, it was time to make a decision, the question put to us was, "Do you want to return to earth with special powers, or without? The next question we will ask you is, do you want to stay in the spirit world and not learn any further?" Patricia and I decided to return to planet Earth once again as twins with paranormal powers.

We were informed by the Ascended Masters that whenever we cut ourselves, we would astound people by our rapid healing, the bleeding would immediately stop and not even a scar will remain, this would happen within seconds after being hurt. We would be in a position where gravity would not keep us earth bound, if we desired to fly, without magic powers or optical illusions, it would happen. People would gather by the thousands to see us do what they call miracles. We will become multimillionaires, but when that happens, we must always think of the less fortunate and unselfishly help them. Patricia and I agreed to these conditions. "Now the next thing;" The Ascended Masters said was, "What kind of parents do you want?" "We want to be of Royal descent again, and free to do as we desire," "No, that will not work for you, we will send you both to a family of billionaires, there you will be able to excel in you special gifts, but you must first attend the necessary schooling. We will send guides to lead you to the right people, and you will be surrounded by angels, keep contact and continually pray, the Ancient of Times will receive a report on a regular basis. Now what names do you desire to have? Tell me and I will prepare your mother; she will pick this up telepathically. You will be happy in this life; there will be love, peace and success." "We would like to be named Vera and Jillian," "Patricia you will be named Vera and you Louise, Jillian. Remember, you will have equal powers and will work together as a team. Go now, you are about to enter someone's womb and become embryos." With this, we found ourselves once again in a dark place cocooned in a seed. We began to grow, the time had arrived for us to be born, once again into a world of luxury, and this time Vera would have a different attitude. We never remembered our previous lives but experienced many a de ja vu.

Years passed, we were both educated at the best school. It was only then we began to realize we had special powers, this happened when Vera was involved in a serious motor accident. When she was taken from the wreck she was severely cut and bleeding, the paramedics, told she had to be hospitalized, and she needed stitches. Whilst they were busy cleaning her wounds, she healed before their eyes. This caused a sensation, "This is unbelievable!" they said, "Never before have we seen anything like this. A cut as deep as that just to heal, we must get a second opinion," with that they lifted her onto the trolley and pushed her into the ambulance. Our lives were beginning to change. We never remembered our conversation with the Ascended Masters, but, instinctively knew we were different from the people with whom we associated.

One winter's morning; Vera and I decided to go skating on a nearby lake, I decided to drive to our destination, we sat on a bench nearby the lake and watched the children skate, Vera and I were deep in thought, suddenly Vera said, "I wonder what it would be like if we could just lift off this bench and float through the air?" "Anything is possible if we believe we can do it, let us just concentrate on this and see what happens," I said. We began to concentrate, we felt ourselves levitate. There was a gasp from the skaters who observed us floating in the air, "How can they do that?" they asked one another.

A few days passed, Vera and I received an invitation to a live show, the producer wanted us to participate, he heard we could float through the air supernaturally and he was willing to pay whatever we determined.

The auditorium was filled with an inquisitive audience, amongst them were many sceptics. Vera and I were cut by one of the audience, we healed within seconds, the next thing we did; was float around the auditorium. We asked for two volunteers, we told them to sit on straight back chairs. Vera and I concentrated; the chairs levitated and floated around the auditorium, "EEEK PUT US DOWN!!" They screamed. This was fun; Vera and I were enjoying this new discovery. We were in great demand; money poured in, to be able to travel to different countries with all expenses paid had become our life style. We were too busy to have a relationship of any kind. The next experience we had was to heal thousands of people, this made us even more popular, we realized the need, and changed our performance to one of healing, our special gifts were never lost, and we were unique until the day we died. We lived to ninety eight. Thousands attended our funeral, we had done our share, and helped mankind where ever we could, and it was a most fulfilling life any twin could experience.

CHAPTER NINE

THE MYSTERY OF THE TOMBS

I had reincarnated once again, Vera had moved on to a different life, her name had changed to Elizabeth, and mine to Etrechia. We were just ordinary citizens who lived comfortably in a lovely home, we were prosperous, and money was plentiful.

A trip to Egypt was advertised, unknown, to me Elizabeth and I booked our seats on the same flight. As fate would have it, we shared the same room in the hotel.

We were all exhausted from the journey; our leader informed us dinner would be served two hours later. This news pleased Elizabeth and I, we could have a little rest, and still be ready in time.

After dinner, we were informed that a trip to the Sphinx would be first on the list, after which we would visit Luxor and see the twin statues of Rameses ll.

We would be served an early breakfast, and the bus would be ready to depart at eight a.m. if anyone arrived late, they would be left behind.

The guide and our leader sat in the front sharing the same seat, we journeyed for miles, and it was well advised to wear our sunglasses, as the sun beating down on the desert sands created a glare. It was not yet eight thirty, and it felt as though the sun would melt the bus. At last we arrived at the stop that took us to the Sphinx, "Unfortunately, we will have to walk, it is advisable to use your sun umbrellas and hats." The guide informed us in broken English.

In spite of the news we had just received, our spirits were not dampened.

"This great giant you see, has a great history," the guide said, he took a deep breath and stood silent for a moment, he gave me the impression he was lost for words, and then continued to talk, "First we will discuss its measurements; this Lion's body is 240 feet long and 66 feet high, its human face is 13 feet wide. Under this great giant are passages and many rooms, I am allowed to take you down a few passages but not into the rooms, once we have seen this, we shall return to the bus and go to luxor to see the twin statues.

This great giant seemed to look right through us; its eyes were alive, some how it was a de ja vu. "I am sure we have been here before," Elizabeth whispered in my ear. "Yes, I feel the same; it must have been in our past lives." At that moment, I regressed, in a vision, I saw Elizabeth and I with many others humming, the Sphinx levitating, this excited me. I returned from the past and turning to Elizabeth said, "We were both here; we were two of the team who brought the Sphinx here. This vision was so real. I wonder what we are going to see and feel next?" "I never regressed, but I could sense what you just told me is true." Elizabeth and I stared at each other; in spite of the desert heat, cold shivers ran down our spines, we began to listen intently to what the guide told us.

We were led to the side of the Sphinx where a door stood open, we climbed the steps and entered a dark passage, from which many passages branched off.

The guide instructed us to use our torches, this we did, strange writings were on the walls, and fortunately the guide knew the way; as he had obviously guided many touring groups.

Ever since this hybrid creature was given its foreign name, the Great Sphinx at Gezeh; has represented to strangers all that are strange and inscrutable about the civilization of ancient Egypt.

Nothing about the great Sphinx is more certain, or harder to comprehend than its tremendous age. According to an ancient text, a young prince riding in the desert paused to nap in the shade of the Sphinx. As he slept the Sphinx spoke to him promising him Egypt's throne if he would remove the sand that had piled up around the statue. The prince Thutumose the lV; did clear the sand and he indeed became King of Egypt 34 centuries ago.

The tour to the Sphinx was exciting, if only we could have stayed a little longer and we felt there was much more to show us; but I suppose they specified a time for each place we were to see as there was much to do in a short time.

We were travelling to Luxor, the journey from the Sphinx, was one of great discussion. Once again it felt as though the extreme heat would not only melt the bus but all the passengers, fortunately each had a fan above their seats, for this we were grateful.

"I wonder why all these tombs were built?" I said loud enough for the guide to hear. "The reason for these tombs is a question many ask. To begin I will give you a little information about the people of Egypt, they believe life everlasting for the Egyptian Pharaohs' was the sustaining principle of their civilization. In an ancient religious text, a deceased king asks of the creator-god "O Atum; what is my duration of life?" And the deity replies, "Thou are destined for millions of millions of years, a life time of millions." "So to supply the necessities for the life times of millions, the kings designed tombs and mortuary temples that would last forever. The common designation for the tomb in fact meant (HOUSE OF ETERNITY.)

As we entered the tomb, we noticed twin statues, and on our right was a large platform with hieroglyphs of the Kings formal names and titles. The tombs have kept alive the names of the ancient kings. They believe to speak their names was to make them alive again." I believed every word I read in the tomb, and wondered whether it applied to us as well.

Our leader told us we would be visiting the Temple of Isis the following day, this information, excited us. That night, sleep did not come easily; I lay awake wondering whether Elizabeth and I knew each other in one of our past lives.

Another question I had to ask myself as the hours ticked by was "Why do I feel as though I had known Elizabeth before? We seemed to understand each other, it was uncanny, we thought alike and had the same interests, experienced the same emotions. Is it possible we were here before? Who knows? We may receive the answers to these questions before we are to return home."

At last in the early hours of the morning, I fell asleep, only to dream of Isis and the stars. Now why should I have dreamt this? I wondered when I awoke.

The Temple of Isis was beautiful, it had large pillars. A statue of Isis stood on a large slab of marble. Elizabeth and I looked at her eyes, they seemed to come alive.

Suddenly we found ourselves in another dimension, Isis stood beside us, she took us by the hand and we flew into the sky, reaching Leo, we looked down to see the Sphinx, on and on we flew, among the stars, "You my two earthlings, were incarnate angels, we were friendly at that time. We spent many hours in the garden of Osiris my husband. I knew you before Lucifer's rebellion. Your names carried the attribute of the Ancient of Times, come I will take you once more to the constellations." This was wonderful, now I have my answers. "There will be more questions answered tomorrow, when you go to Horus' temple, when you return, your lives will never be the same, enjoy this time we have together, who knows when we will be able to spend time together again. Now I must return you to your group."

As suddenly as we found ourselves floating in the air, we were back in the temple with Isis staring down at us with a little smile on her lips.

Elizabeth and I sat in silence most of the journey back to the hotel.

The following day we went to the Temple of Horus, and wondered what awaited us.

CHAPTER TEN

THE UNDERWORLD

The guide took us down a dark passage beneath the temple of Horus, his voice faded away, Elizabeth and I held hands we felt nervous and somehow knew we were not alone.

"Do not be afraid," we heard someone say, turning around, we saw an apparition; it had the body of a man and a head of a jackal. "I am Anubis, the god of the underworld, and I am about to show you where the spirits of the kings and queens live. Just follow me." We stared at him wide eyed, and still feeling nervous and afraid we followed him into a room.

Many kings and queens sat on thrones, they wore their Royal robes. "Why are they sitting here? And how long have they been here?" "For hundreds of years, they are not willing to move on. They want to remain king; they are bound to the underworld. If they do not choose to move on shortly after they have left their bodies, they remain here in prison in the state they were when they died. I Anubis make sure they do not leave this place until they decide to move on. Come I will show you where the famous Pharaohs' are" He led us down another passage; "Menes founded the city of Memphis 20 miles south of the Apex of the Delta, near where the regions of Lower and Upper Egypt meet, and established it as his capital. The city was destined to become the greatest in the land. He could not let the idea of being king go. Come, I will show you his throne room."

Anubis opened the door of the room in which Menes sat on his throne, "In the inter leading room his successes some 18 kings of two successive dynasties that spanned over about 400 years ruled from here. They all have their throne rooms, and they refuse to give up their thrones. With the result, they will be prisoners of their own choice. Many lives await them, but they refuse to let go."

Elizabeth and I looked at these pitiful specimens. "If only they would just let go of the past," Elizabeth said "Yes, there is so much more for them to do than to sit here for all eternity just hoping their kingdom will return." Anubis added.

"Now we will go to a section of a well known and loved Pharaoh his name was Thutmose 111 his wife's name was Hatsheput. One of the surest proofs of Hatsheput's greatness was her ability to keep a man Of Thutmose 111demensions under her thumb for so long. Thutmose had brains, vision and drive; he was to become the Alexander the Great of Egypt, the creator of Egypt's empire. Yet for 20 years he lived in the shadow of a strong minded woman who was his stepmother and his aunt. Finally he gathered the backing he needed to unseat her. Now she sits here in the underworld alone in her chamber and Thutmose

111 in his. Both tried to destroy each other, now both still are trying to reign." The spirit of sadness and desperation filled their chambers, it had such a divesting effect upon Elizabeth and I, and we began to cry. "Do not weep, they are only here because they chose to be;" Anubis said. "Come, there is still one more Pharaoh I would like you to see.

We walked what seemed for miles down many passages, and began to wonder whether we would find our way back to the group. Anubis read our thoughts "Do not be concerned about returning to your group, I will escort you. Now we are entering a very sacred tomb, but, you must first pass the goddess Serket, she is protecting the tomb of King Tutankhamen, they have removed many parts of his body and placed them under the protection of many gods. The only part that was not removed was his heart. Now here we are, see his body is still encased in his golden coffin. He was more popular than Thutmose 111. And I believe he will go down in history for all eternity. Come now, I must return you to the group". Within seconds, we were back in the entrance hall with the group.

"What an experience that was," I said, "Yes it was," Elizabeth agreed.

We returned to the hotel with the feeling of a deep satisfaction we had learned about the tombs. The following day we flew back to our own country.

Not many days after our arrival at home, there was an earth quake; Elizabeth and I were flung once again into space, where we found ourselves floating among the stars.

The Ancient of times summoned all who had died in the earthquake and enquired of us whether we would like to return to earth in another human form or remain in the spirit to help humans from the celestial plain or the earthly plain. We both decided to remain spirits and help the humans from the earthly plain. The Angel in charge of the records told the Ancient of Times, we qualified to be Ascended Masters and could work from the Celestial and Earthly plain. This news pleased us, and here we now are, Ascended Masters, helping those who have to go through the trials of life. We would not have it any other way.

CHAPTER ELEVEN

THE JUDGING CHAMBER

Elizabeth and I were shown into a large room, in which stood three desks, and four large armchairs. A large screen covered nearly three quarters of a wall, this was used to replay the lives of the newly crossed over. There the decision was made by the ascended Masters where the souls were to be sent after their cleansing. Their past lives were totally wiped from their memories, and a new life began. Many were sent to other planets and others back to earth, they became seeds in a woman's womb were fertilized and later were born to start life over. Some could choose to return and others had no choice. The Ascended Masters told them there were lessons to be learnt. Many returned rather reluctantly, unfortunately this had to take place for the souls to perfect themselves.

Elizabeth and I attended classes; we were training to become Ascended Masters, even though we sat in at the judgments there was still much to learn.

We were near the time to write our first exam, when a very interesting case arrived. His name was

Jack, he was tall and had a rugged look, after he had discarded his earthly clothes and changed into his spiritual robe, he looked completely different, and he had lost his rugged look.

The first question he asked us was, "Am I dead?" The Master who was assigned to be our trainer answered, "You certainly are not on earth at the moment, and you were involved in a car accident. Going home from a party, you took a couple of chances and crashed into a bridge and you landed in a river and drowned." "What will happen to me now?" Jack asked in a pitiful frightened voice. "You will have to stay here for a while and be judged, after which we will decide your fate." Our trainer replied. "Will I never see my family again? What about my wife and children, they are going to be left alone and will have to struggle to survive." "You do not have to worry about them any more, it is too late for that, when you were with them, and you were not someone who took your responsibilities seriously." "Let me go back, give me another chance, please I beg you." "Sorry Jack, it is too late for that now, no matter how much you regret your actions, and there can be no turning back now." Jack's eyes filled with tears, I would not take heed when I was warned. I have been warned countless times not to drink before driving, but of course, I knew better. I know I have been stubborn and became aggressive every time I was warned." Well." Our trainer responded to Jack's confession, "when you have gone through your judgment, you will be sent wherever the Ascended Masters decide. In the mean time, we will show you how you treated your wife and children and colleagues not only whilst you were under the influence of alcohol, but when you were sober."

The Master instructed Elizabeth to switch the DVD on then instructed Jack to watch himself on the screen.

He saw himself arriving home late at night; he had been in the bar for hours. He heard himself cursing as he tripped over his own feet; he dragged his sleeping wife out of bed and began beating her unmercifully. Her screams woke the children, they stood screaming, and he turned on his children and began to beat them with his belt. His children ran out of the house to a neighbour to get help, they called the police who arrived to see him beating his wife until she fell unconscious. They arrested him on the charges of assault, abuse and attempted murder. He witnessed his wife being taken to hospital by ambulance. His children were taken to their grand mother; there they remained until his wife was discharged from the hospital. Jack saw himself in prison, this scene was repeated many times, then the accident, now here he was, he had no idea where. "How do you feel about witnessing yourself behaving in such a way?" Jack was asked by our trainer, "Terrible!! Switch that DVD off I do not want to see any more" "I am afraid you will have to see every thing you did good and bad" our trainer exclaimed. This was too stressful for Jack, he wept bitterly, "I did not realize I was so cruel, my poor wife and children, how they must have feared me. I think they must be relieved I am dead." "Well, they no longer live in fear of what might happen when you come home." This made Jack cry even more bitterly. "Oh God! What have I done!! What have I done!!"

he fell to his knees and wept even more bitterly than before. "That will be all for today," our trainer said. "Tomorrow, you must return and we will continue from where we left off." Elizabeth and I accompanied Jack to his room. He threw himself on his bed and wept as though his heart would break in half. "What have I done!!? What have I done!!?" he buried his face in his pillow and wept until he fell asleep totally exhausted.

CHAPTER TWELVE

THE LORDS OF KARMA

The following morning after breakfast, Elizabeth and I were instructed to accompany Jack to the Judgment room. After he was seated, our instructor entered, followed by the Lords of Karma.

They were stern looking men; it was obvious they were carrying out their duties for many years.

Our instructor told me to switch the DVD on. Jack witnessed his own funeral. He counted ten people at his grave side. Besides his family and the preacher only his employer was there. Jack gave a gasp, "I did not realize I was so disliked," he said mournfully. "As a man lives, so shall he die, and as a tree falls, so shall it lie." One of the Lords of Karma said. Elizabeth was instructed to push the back button; this took us into the office in which Jack worked. It showed one morning in particular, Jack was suffering from a hang over, he was very aggressive. One colleague was sent to fetch a couple of documents from Jack's office, "What do you want?" Jack snarled at this youngster who was obeying orders from his superiors. "Sir, I have come to fetch documents, they are needed upstairs." Jack picked up the files in which the documents were and threw them across the office. The young man bent to pick them up, Jack lost his temper and kicked the young man who lost his balance and fell hitting his head on the corner of the desk. Blood squirted out, the cut was deep, and Jack phoned the dispensary and asked the first aid controller to help this young man. When Jack was questioned, he was angry and retorted "This youngster was insolent, and deserved what he got, I demand respect." He shouted. There were many such out bursts of anger before that day; Jack was the most unpopular man on the staff. That morning he was given a warning, his employer walked into his office with the Personal Manager; "If this happens again, you will be dismissed immediately" Jack was told. He could not believe what he saw. "Are you sure that you were looking at me?" One incident after another took place, each was becoming steadily worse. "Well, there is only one thing for you," the Lord of Karma said, "You will return to earth, your parents will abuse you, they will beat you, and you will be disliked by everyone, if you do not desire to change your attitude, you will have to repeat that kind of life until you do."

Jack fell to his knees, "Please! Do not send me back to suffer like that," "Remember what you did to your wife and children, they suffered under your hand, now it is your turn to have the same fate." With that the Lord of Karma turned to Elizabeth and me and instructed us to accompany Jack to his room and help him prepare for his journey back to earth and his new parents.

The following soul to be led into the judgment chamber was a young girl named Maria who too had suffered abuse and was killed by her father.

Her DVD showed her crying and in prayer, she saw herself on her knees by her bed, "Oh God, please help me, take me away from this place, even though I am being abused, show my dad what he is doing is wrong, he has raped me and beaten me help me to escape from here, I know that if he caught me trying to run away he will kill me. Please God help me!!!" That night, she packed her clothes and began tip toeing to the front door as she passed her father's room, the door opened and her father came out with a large stick, he began beating Maria, she lost her balance and fell to the floor, blood splattered everywhere, she screamed for help but no one arrived to help her, she saw her father beating her, as she watched the DVD she burst into tears, "Am I going to be punished because I tried to run away?" she asked," No my child," the Lord of Karma answered, "You will be sent to parents who will love and care for you all their lives, they will be God loving and you will have a happy and successful life. It is time for your departure; go now in peace, your new life awaits you." With that, Maria dried her tears and said "Thank you, I am grateful for what you are doing for me." The Lord of Karma smiled at her and stood watching as she walked down the passage towards the transport that stood waiting for the souls who were destined to return to earth that day.

Every day was a new experience for Elizabeth and I, our training became more intense, we did not mind because we wanted to be good and trusted Ascended Masters.

A new soul arrived an elderly man named William, all his life he loved people and animals, he did his best to please everyone, his life was filled with prayer, from a tiny child he loved to pray and as he grew older he taught others to pray, many lives changed because of his lifestyle when he breathed his last, it was done with a song of praise on his lips.

His reward was to join the student ASCENDED MASTERS, what a better reward could there be?

When we pass over to the other side, we do not know what awaits us. If we want to experience a peaceful life in our new spiritual home, we must take stock now of our attitudes and behaviour toward our fellow man.

Life on this earth can be wonderful if we live helping and blessing others,

And once we have reached the place where it is no longer necessary for us to return we can look at our heavenly records and say, "I did my best and ran a good race and won. That is what I desire for everyone who reads this book".